FLATLINE

FLATLINE

[AND THE ANTS DREAM OF THE NEW WORLD ORDER]

K. M. Williams

Song lyrics by Ed Pastorini - BMI Copyright
2003 - Used with permission.
All rights reserved.

Copyright 2026

LCCN 2025924558

ISBN 979-8-9937797-7-5 (pb)
ISBN 979-8-9937797-8-2 (hc)
ISBN 979-8-9937797-2-0 (ebook)

Cover and interior design by CoverKitchen

For info, write Kindness, Inc. 5915 Charlotte
Street, KCMO 64110, USA

Email: krayonkcmo@gmail.com

Kindness, Inc.

First Edition – Printed in the United States of America

LOTTO

The first thing I learned is that I'd won a Lottery and my Revival was the prize. The Revival was strange—and mundane. And unexpected; I mean, it went in an unexpected direction. At first, I was eager to see my prize and then ...

Once my eyes opened, I regained consciousness quickly. I was given a monochrome jumpsuit to wear. After sensory rehab and practice moving my limbs, I regained mobility. I could walk! Now, I really wanted to get out of this windowless Storage facility. The monitoring devices were removed, and I was put in an institutional cell with only a bed and an attached swivel tray for meals: food pills, nondescript edibles—bland.

I could think, I was cognitive, and my senses worked, but when they held up a mirror, I didn't recognize my reflection. I was terrified. I tried to remember my life, to picture it, myself, anything; I wracked my brains.

Nothing. I tried smiling, but it looked like a grimace. I grinned, but that didn't work either. My head was the correct size for an adult of maybe twenty-five or so, with big ears. My haircut was short, shorn. My eyebrows were like exclamation points, my lips skinny. I leaned closer (hazel eyes), and even when I pulled back, I seemed to stare. An unblinking gaze, perhaps from overwhelming surprise.

"I can't remember my life," I said. "I recognize most *things*, but there's no context. I don't recognize *myself*."

I could identify things, names came to me, sometimes even within a kind of vague memory. But there was no context. It was as if the things were in a container and I couldn't remember anything beyond it.

Three Storage Facility staff were assigned to me, remarkably like humans. All three had androgynous features, and one had big curly doll-like eyelashes. Supposed to read female? Their mouths didn't move, their speech emanated from somewhere else; I couldn't figure it out. And there was a delay before responses, which lacked affect. Disconcerting and ugly. So far, they'd offered zero backstory to my previous existence. They were oversized, half a head taller than me, with large hands. 'Bouncer' popped into my head, a random image of weaponized AI bots—a memory?

One day, they escorted me to a sub-storage chamber and stood facing me in a semi-circle.

One broke the seal on a metallic box on a cart and opened the lid.

"What's this?" I asked. Every time I used my voice,

it startled me. I rasped; a hoarse off-pitch, foreign tone. How many years had it been since I'd spoken? How long had I been in 'storage?'

"Worldly possessions." The voice sounded like it came out of a tin can.

I looked inside. There was a pair of sneakers, a small rectangular box with lettering and a silhouette illustration of a kid, a vertical folded thingy, two tubes at the bottom: one green with a strap and one a metallic canister. And a small rectangular screen with a red border, two knobs, and the words 'Etch-A-Sketch.'

I held up the Etch-A-Sketch. "What's this?"

"Antique toy."

"I've never seen it before." I put it back in the box and took out the folded triangle thingy. It opened into a cap attached to a miniature umbrella. The umbrella part was a sandy color.

"I recognize this, sort of," I said. "Like an umbrella hat. A cheap novelty for party favors." I put it back.

Next, I picked up the canister, a tube of about ten inches, labeled 'Time Capsule.' I tried to open it, unscrew the cap, but it didn't budge. Then I noticed a slot and a series of digits and letters on the side. I pressed the digits in a random sequence—nothing.

"Do you know the code? What's the code?"

"Lock code," said a voice.

I rolled my eyes. "Are you sure this is *my* Time Capsule? My box of ... of junk toys?" I waved my hand at the contents. "I don't recognize any of this."

"Shipped with your storage body."

I let out a breath. "Are you robots or what? Clones, hybrids—??"

Figuring it was the ringleader, I turned to the one with eyelashes.

"Who's doing the talking? Who's in charge?"

The eyelashes one spoke; its mouth actually moved, like a ventriloquist's dummy.

"We are citizens. The present matters most."

The mouth stopped moving. Then closed and opened again. **"Cause of death: Unknown, possible hit-and-run bike accident. Body complete at time of storage."**

Mouth pulled a brochure from a pocket and held it out to me. Bullet points read: Report Memory Loss or Brain Trauma. Regrowing Memories. Upcoming Death. Maintaining a Diary.

Definitely robots. Dumb AI machines. I wanted to brain all three of them. I stifled the urge. They were my only source of info. I was outnumbered anyway.

Mouth informed me: **"Next steps: 1. Deliver to Shelter. 2. Examination, assessment, and possible restoration. 3. Escort to assigned habitat in Shelter."**

The *shelter* part had me worried. Along with my Return, they informed me that I'd won a future habitat as part of my Lottery prize—a moderately sized mansion! So, since this was the future—it might be even better than the mansions I knew ... or worse ... But what choice did I have? I asked to see my original habitat, where I'd lived when I was alive, along with the prize one. It might help me remember my life. They stood still, blank.

"N/A."

"Not Applicable," Mouth echoed, then guffawed, or laughed, what was supposed to be a laugh—more like a donkey hee-haw. **"Original habitat gone. Detour to prize location but not a living option."**

Now I was really worried.

I started talking to myself, in my head. I was escorted down a corridor to an entry ramp, a gangplank, along with the cart—and box of possessions. They had me boxed in, but I felt eager and ready to get a glimpse of the outside world! But, no—we boarded through a hatch-port into a small sealed cabin with a single seat—and no windows. The mute bots pointed for me to sit, handed me the box, and exited. That left Mouth, who stood next to my seat. I sensed motion.

"In Transit."

I tried not to panic. I figured we were traveling in some version of a self-driving spinner; it hovered and flew.

"What country are we in, or city?" I asked.

"No countries."

"I used to live in New York City, The United States, America."

"Kaput." Mouth's mouth opened, laughed, another donkey hee-haw. Then clamped shut, opened again. **"Nope."** But the mouth didn't close, it was stuck open. A glitch?

"Are there other people who've come back to life? I'd like to meet someone—to talk to—?"

"Sampling of species returned. Various epochs. Archives. All gone, except you. Last one. Facility closing soon."

That did not sound promising. I closed my eyes, feeling exhausted.

When I opened them, I was alone. Mouth had gone still, inert, mouth stuck open. Maybe I'd fallen asleep, but I couldn't tell how much time had elapsed. The hatch port opened, a strange light flooding in.

I stood up and went out. My prize-winning mansion was a vacant lot with an empty concrete hole, like an old swimming pool. I looked around. There was nothing except dust, mud and sand swirling across concrete. Microchips were scattered everywhere like seeds. The sky was a hazy yellowish color. Polluted? The air had an artificial chemical smell. Was I in a dome? Maybe everyone lived in domes now. The air was hot then chilly, the temperature cycling between dry hot/cold extremes. I wondered how it felt at night.

The landscape ahead was mainly flat desert and low warehouse-type buildings, most bunkered into the earth. I peered at the horizon and saw an irregular dark outline, maybe a city or town in the distance, but it was hard to be sure. I turned a circle. Vacant lots and holes, as far as the eye could see. An empty abandoned landscape; wafting sand, concrete. An eclipse of the sun came to mind, a dim, silent earth. No birds, no sound, no signs of life.

I went back to the transit chamber and sat down. The hatch closed and the gizmo started up. I sensed movement, but without orientation, I lost track of time again—floating, just floating ... Everything felt like an apparition. I was beginning to feel like one too. I wondered if I was on Earth.

Abruptly, all motion ceased. The hatch opened again. I stood up—fingers crossed, I thought—and went out. A female figure approached, probably another human proxy. This one wore a nametag: *Allegra Geller* – Guide.

"Welcome to the shelter," she said. A high-pitched chirpy voice and toothy smile. But she looked and spoke like a human. So, Allegra G. was an upscale AI model, with a name and gender.

I faced a large decrepit structure of cracks and crumbling stone. The façade was riddled with break lines, and chipped; whole chunks missing. There was scroll work below a stone roof, one collapsing column and a partial one, on either side of the façade. Wide stairs spanned the building to the entrance: rusted metal doors with small windows. On either side of the stairs stood a dirty gray statue of a lion; one was headless.

"What is this place?"

"Lost Millennium architecture, a 'Library,'" Allegra said. "Storage for written words, books mostly. To read or borrow and return."

"I know what a library is."

"Condemned." She grinned. She actually grinned.

A distinct memory came to me: the Library Lions at

the main NYC Public Library. Except this building was crumbling. The NYC one covered an entire city block, but this one was shrunken—the roof had sunk on one side. Beyond it was an outline of surrounding streets, no buildings. Cityscape as excavation site, ruins ... it didn't feel like NYC.

We entered the building. The interior was a dim, cavernous space. We passed two floor signs: *Grand Hall* and *Restoration* with an arrow pointing to a set of stairs going down.

"You must be thirsty," she said. We stopped at a podium with a Guest Book. She handed me a canister. Taking a drink, I followed her down the stairs.

I'd gone to a concert with friends, but lost them.
I couldn't remember how we'd gotten there, or
where to go to find them so I could get home. It
had gotten dark quickly. I saw some buildings on
a hill ahead, so I went to see if I could get some
help, ask for directions, figure out where I was.
The building was a series of adjoining restaurants
and bars, filled with rowdy people, concertgoers,
locals. I had my bag, money, and wallet, but no
phone. I must have left it at home. I kept asking
for directions, the nearest transit station, but no
one could give me any info. In fact, they mostly
just ignored me. I started walking faster, speeding
up. I could feel myself panic, my head spinning.
No one would help me. I went from one party bar
to the next; it was just a long, endless building.

Finally, I gave up, got out of there. I started
walking. Maybe I could find my friends or a
transit entrance. It was so dark I couldn't tell
where I was. I kept walking and walking. Soon I
was following transit tracks. I wondered if I was
on the West Side, close to the river, but I couldn't
see it. The night was inky black, only a few dim
streetlights. I didn't know which direction I was
going in, or even what city I was in—maybe I was
in NYC, way north, but the landscape started
to look almost rural at the edges, like historical
pictures of NYC when it was first settled.

Maybe I was trudging north, I couldn't tell.
I was desperate to come to a park or some
residential area or find somebody, anybody
who could steer me towards a transit entrance.
I went up a hill street. At the top, I looked
around, but it all looked the same. Maybe
I'd gone in a circle. I turned around.

Up another hill, with small houses and
yards, I came across a street in a run-down
neighborhood. There were no sidewalks, just
a single streetlight. The houses were shabby,
shadowy, only one with dim lights inside. I
heard voices, but it was too dark to see anyone.

I stood for a moment, thinking. Could I get
even more lost? I was really tired from walking,
not knowing which way to go. Suddenly, a
pair of figures came out of the shadows under
a streetlight. Teenagers, a boy and a girl.

"Hey," I called. "Do you know where
the nearest transit station is?"

The guy pointed behind them without
stopping. "A couple blocks ..." They
disappeared into the darkness.

"Thanks," I said, but they were gone.

I started walking in the direction he'd pointed.
Back down the hill. The whole neighborhood
was deserted—buildings, warehouses, an
industrial area. I kept walking but the street I
was on didn't lead anywhere. No people, street
activity, stores—everything was closed and dark.
Dark, deserted streets, dark like at the outer
edges of a city, where everything dissolves into
nothing. I wondered if the teenagers had given
me wrong directions just to mess with me.

I spotted two people ahead in the darkness,
on a bench in front of a boarded-up building.
I went up to them. They looked homeless
or like vagrants. They acted sort of friendly,
invited me to sit, making a space for me on the
bench. But I was afraid, there was something
off about them. I could tell they were sizing
me up. I sat down, asked about the nearest
transit station, but got up again, almost
immediately. They stood up too, said they were
taking off, and wished me luck. After they left,
I realized that they'd distracted me, gotten
into my bag, taken my wallet, money, ID.

Now I was really lost. I'd gotten lost, I
was lost again. Lost, with nothing.

I remembered nothing of the Restoration. When I came to, I was lying on a bed in a room. Time had passed, I guess. Had I been asleep—or in some kind of delirium? I couldn't remember dreaming.

I sat up and looked around. The bed was horizontal against a wall that showed an AI rendering of a night table and lamp. The headboard, another AI rendering, was a half-wall to an alcove facing a door. I got up and went over, but the door was locked. I knocked, but nothing. To the left was a built-in wardrobe—more monochrome jumpsuits on hangers. All they needed was a number stamped on the back to qualify as prison uniforms. One drawer at the bottom with a few undergarments. Across from the wardrobe was a bathroom: sink, mirror, toilet, shower; basic but real.

The entire wall on the far side of the room was a kitchen "mural," an AI job: fridge, stove, sink and counter in a line. Above the sink, a cupboard and window with curtains—looking out to an AI view of a tree and sky. A small round table and chair stood in front of the kitchen, a Mr. Coffee maker on top with supply packets, cups, and a brochure.

Across from the bed was an easy chair. I tried it, and surprise—it was comfortable. The chair was angled to a flat wall screen, like an old Smart TV. The remote was attached on the side and wouldn't come off. I pressed ON anyway, and a weather channel appeared: graphics and a pulsing background of current temperature, windspeed, etc. I tried scrolling, but the screen kept coming up blank.

Behind the easy chair was a wall shelf with a jigsaw puzzle of Pinocchio (it turned out to have missing pieces), fake flowers in a vase, a yo-yo—? and a feather duster.

The front of the room was wall-to-wall floor-length curtains. I went to open them, looking on both sides, but they didn't open. I tugged and managed to peek out. I looked out across a hall to more glass display-size windows. I cupped my eyes to peer out, but no luck. It was too dim to discern anything except closed curtains. Since rising from the storage, I'd not seen a single window except these. The only outside I'd experienced was the vacant mansion lot and the stairs from the transit shuttle to the shelter.

All of the furnishings were throwback styles of non-specific eras. A mashup of Old Millennium, from the 1950s... "Kaput" was the right way to describe it. My habitat was a box, with all the character of a generic chain motel. Some jackpot. The whole set-up devised from algorithms, by an AI content creator/team mimicing vintage Cyber Life.

I went to look at the brochure next to Mr. Coffee. The text read: "Returnees are housed here to give Visitors—historians, researchers, reporters & tour groups—a rare and authentic glimpse of humanoids who inhabited Earth, *once upon a time.* Enjoy this unique experience of historical earthlings and humanoid hybrid species in their original habitat!*

One-on-one meetings can be arranged by appointment for an additional Donation to the Museum of Earthly Delights."

So. I was now living in a museum, in my very own

'vintage' diorama. I spotted a call box next to the display glass and made a beeline for it. I cranked up the volume to Max and pressed Speak. My voice came booming out:

"HOW LONG DO I HAVE TO STAY HERE?"

No answer.

I couldn't believe it—my new life was to be an exhibit in some run-down Earth museum—my planet, my home, where I'd been alive and lived. And obviously where no one else (really) lived anymore. My second chance at life. No wonder the extinct 'Earthlings' kept the curtains closed. I felt like throwing a tantrum. I wanted to bang on the door, the walls—but what good would it do? I turned a circle and plopped into the easy chair, my eyes filling with tears. I sat for a long time, crying and sniffling. *The Day the Earth Stood Still* popped into my head. My memory might be vague, but now I had one real desire: to get the hell out of this place. I wiped my face with my arm, got up, and went to the call box:

"I want to meet a real human."

The curtains opened suddenly the next day. They were rigged to an auto-day/night timer, along with the display window glass—transparent or tinted. More props/ faux décor. And the weather channel was a loop, always the same.

Days passed and no Visitors came to the Museum. Robots removed the call box. Museum staff, bot guards, delivered meals, Memos and Request forms. Meals were in boxes with a tantalizing realistic picture of the food, e.g. a plate with turkey, steaming mashed potatoes with butter and string beans, but inside were compressed lumps.

The Request forms: I could fill one out and ask for *things*—they never answered *questions*. They sent surveys though, tons of them. After a week, I tossed them in a corner and wrote a Request for a trash can. *Things* were delivered to my door by the bot guards. None could talk. Or so it seemed. I started calling them all 'Gort' and talked to them sometimes, filling in their answers. The jumpsuits annoyed me. They were all XX. I filled out a Request for scissors and cut a couple pairs in half to make pants and tops. I Requested a T-shirt and sweatpants, since I never went anywhere, but only got the jumpsuits.

One day, I tried on the sneakers in the possessions box and—they fit! I stuffed the Storage Facility sandals in the trash slot and wore Whoever's sneakers. The first few days, I spent hours trying to crack the Time Capsule code. No luck, no way. Infinite possibilities. I stuck it back in the box. Then I looked at the green tube with *L.L. Bean* lettering. Something tickled my memory. That cap opened. Inside were sections of a fishing rod and reel, and a packet: one leader, one line, two hooks and a fly. I tried to remember, draw up a specific memory, but nothing. I set the flyrod and reel aside, closed up the box, stashed it in the wardrobe, and forgot about it.

I was lonely. I wanted to go out—*anywhere!* Just for a few minutes. None of the curtains across the Grand Hall opened. I never heard a peep. I wondered if any living thing had ever lived there. I wrote down my experiences from the first day of my Revival. I wanted to write down my dreams, but I could never remember any. Maybe I didn't dream anymore. I wondered about my 'Restoration'—what they'd done to me. I put in a Request for the records and received one page, redacted or blank. An age estimate showed a range between twenty and twenty-eight, and there was an empty box labeled *Microchip*. I went in the bathroom, checked my entire body for signs of chips or insertions and found none. But who knew what surveillance devices they used now. I kept trying to remember my Restoration sleep/dream, but only drew a blank. I slept a lot, took naps, worn out from worry. Other times, I'd just burst into laughter, in disbelief. I needed to escape— maybe stage a rebellion.

I submitted Requests daily. Questions and demands for answers mainly: How long would I be there? When would I go outside? Requests for jumpsuits with colors, food with flavors, real flowers, the missing Pinocchio jigsaw pieces—whatever I could think of. I still couldn't remember my name, so I signed the requests 'Lotto.'

I was granted permission to start an ant farm.

Most Requests were returned: N/A. There were no paintings on the walls, no music sources. I started humming to myself.

The ants were delivered in a typical farm, a two-sided see-through glass rectangle. Black ants. I liked watching them travel through their tunnels with purpose. 'Klaatu' popped into my head. I could name myself 'Klaatu,' as a joke. But there was nobody to get it. A humorless, mute world. So I named the ants the Klaatu Family Farm.

Then one Day Mode, out of the blue, I received a Memo that an investigative journalist was coming to interview me for a feature story. *The Times* Sunday Edition, the Galaxy section, a popular Sunday insert, with a readership of millions (it claimed). I was elated, euphoric—at first. Then I thought, what if the journalist wasn't human? He better be.

FLY-FISHING

Museum – Week?

Time passed, but it didn't feel like it. I was suspended between Time and Space. Looking in the bathroom mirror made me queasy, thinking, one day, I might not see anything. I felt like I was aging, growing deeper frown lines and decided to measure my hair, to see if it was growing. I started a calendar so I wouldn't lose my marbles. No months, just a number grid. Every day I made an X. All of the curtains across the Grand Hall remained closed. No signs of life.

After many Xs, a Gort came to my room and escorted me to 'The Stacks.' I was free to read any of the sparse collection of dusty books. The Stacks: a warehouse of empty shelves. No history, politics, geography, not even encyclopedia sets; so much for non-fiction. The United States, past or present, zero. So, I browsed the travel section, also weird. The places in the books were un-known to me and read like fairy tales. Were they imag-inary, invented chronicles? No explorers, historical or contemporary, like Redmond O' Hanlon. Just cruise bro-chures. The destinations were AI renditions, fantastical, with superheroes and imaginary animals. The most pop-ular cruises didn't actually go anywhere. The mega-ships just docked at piers, offering gambling and AI gamer dis-tractions, plus shopping.

The Stacks were stocked with plenty of romance, unfortunately. A small mystery section—most I'd al-ready read. Luckily, I found a couple Raymond Chan-dlers. I took *The Big Sleep*. Books might stimulate my memory. Or, at least, kill time. I also found a small pile of sheet music on a bottom shelf. Oddly, I knew how to read music! So I started reading and singing the tunes, a mix of genres. I was escorted to the Stacks each week. The Gorts always stationed themselves at the entrance. When I left, they counted the books I took out. Program-ming. Go figure.

Near the end of another interminable, indomitable X, I glanced up from reading and saw a slight movement of a curtain in a diorama kitty-corner from mine. I did a double take. The curtain was still. Was my mind play-ing tricks on me?

A little later, the curtains in that diorama opened, the windows turned to Day Mode, and I could see in-side. I went closer to get a better look. The room was a mirror of mine, the same layout, same furnishings, but of a different era. Then the door in the back opened and Allegra-Guide escorted a guy inside. She left, and he was alone. The guy was thin and tall, with short black hair. He wore track pants, a T-shirt with a possum drawing, and hiking boots. He looked fit, maybe younger than me. The main thing was, he looked human! He moved like he was in a daze, turning slowly, gazing around blankly—drugged from his Restoration?

He sat down near the end of the bed and fell back, onto one side. For a while, he lay slumped, then rolled over, his eyes open, staring. And then he saw me. He stood up and came to the front glass. We looked at each other. He had a strange look on his face—surprise? Confusion? I didn't know how I felt; it was literally a lifetime since I'd seen another human. I was elated, dumbfounded. We just stood, looking at each other. I raised my hand and waved. He waved back. I waved again, and he did too. We kept on waving. It made me laugh. My laughter sounded funny, which made me laugh harder. I hadn't laughed since—I couldn't remember. He started laughing too. We both just stood there, laughing and waving. I pressed a hand on the glass, and he did too. I pressed my other hand. And slowly, we started mirroring each other, making gestures, motions, movements, doing different things ... and then, suddenly, just like that, the windows switched to Night Mode—a quick fade to black and he was gone.

I woke up that night in the middle of a dream. I was a student at an art institute, in a studio course with other students. I was chatting with a woman when a tall guy entered—he was unbelievably good-looking. Elvis? Or an Elvis impersonator? A kaleidoscope of movie star faces came to my mind, but I couldn't name them. Anyway, he was in the class and I had to meet him, so I went over to talk. There was something goofy about him, he was kind of a dork. He seemed oblivious to his charm and good looks, which made him even more appealing. Not too perfect.

He offered to show me the basement studios. I immediately fantasized about seduction and intimacy. We went downstairs, roamed around, ending up in a small, quiet studio. Without speaking, we took turns taking our clothes off, and moved toward each other, touching, embracing ... the orgasm I had woke me.

I fell back asleep, but remembered snippets of it in the morning; it was black and white, like an old classic, with close-ups of our faces. Did the dream guy have a name? The guy across the hall popped into my head. He was also good-looking and—of course, I'd dreamed about him. Sex! I'd forgotten all about it. I felt excited, almost cheerful for the first time since my Revival. I fantasized about standing at the window, undressing. But then what—we'd just be voyeurs. I wondered what would happen if I submitted a Request to meet the new Returnee, my neighbor. Or just Request to have sex with him. Ha! I decided to call him 'Guy,' hoping for a chance to hear his real name and his laugh.

Unfortunately, right after the curtains opened and

Day Mode started, a couple of Gorts entered Guy's habitat and escorted him out. His curtains remained open all day, but the room was empty. Back to my celibate exhibit status, verging on extinction.

Another Day/Night X passed but Guy was gone. I wondered what his story was. Our waving was the most fun I'd had since my Revival. Revival. What a joke. It didn't feel like coming back to life. Some jackpot. I was supposed to be a winner. I wondered about my long-term fate. Even if I wanted to cry, I'd run out of tears. At times, fear would strike, taking over my whole body, making me shake. But I was also starting to see, to feel, that I had nothing to lose.

I thought about the journalist, the Investigative Journalist. What would he look like?

INTERVIEW

About four Xs later, the whatchamacallit human, hybrid—Allegra G. arrived with a man who looked human—but—no telling! I mean, I couldn't tell. How was I supposed to know? The journalist, investigative, was about my height and build, with graying wavy brown hair, big owl eyes, goofy black spectacles and chin stubble. He wore a beige car coat over a button-down, khakis and shoes that reminded me of ones called Hush Puppies.

He took a seat in the easy chair, and I sat at my dining table. I don't know why but I immediately felt suspicious of him. Probably because I didn't trust any of the Museum Staff.

"I'm from *The Times*," he said. His voice was deep, a little gravelly.

"Hi," I said. "Are you human?"

He almost smiled. "I try to be. I come from biological humans. And I'm not enhanced."

"Enhanced. What does that mean?"

"One example is DNA enhanced before birth to increase intelligence, longevity. One of many genetic modifications available. Very common these days."

"How old are you?"

"Two hundred, give or take a few years."

I didn't know what to say.

"That's a joke. I'm a Returnee too." He looked at me. "How old are you?"

"I don't know exactly," I said. "No birthdate and I

don't remember much at all about my life. They said I won a Lottery, my Revival was the prize. I don't remember the Lottery, and I don't remember dying. If they know anything, they aren't saying. I'm being held captive here. This place is very secretive. And dull." I didn't know what to say next. I made a smiley face. "Hi! I'm Lotto, short for Lottery! ... I don't know my real name!"

"Really?" He looked at me closely. "Did you ever hear of a Tetra, possibly a robot or clone?"

"Nope," I said. "They said nothing except maybe I died in a bicycle accident, possible head trauma—maybe why my memory is blank. I'm not even sure I died. I mean, maybe I was in a coma or induced coma, and that's when they went and put me in some kind of suspended cryogenic animation state, for my Revival—?"

"They haven't used cryogenics for decades. Revival is the name of the conglomerate who first succeeded in the contemporary methodology. As for the Lottery, they gave out coupons in the beginning. Billionaire CEOs and Venture corps wanted to test it before they invested, so they handed out coupons on the street. Which promised big prizes. Once they knew the process worked, the price tag skyrocketed, and the coupons turned to gold." He kept looking at me. "I'll look into it, your lottery ticket, and your origins. It's part of my job. Maybe I can help you—"

"Can you help me get out of here? I can't stand this place. There's no one alive here. Just cheap robots."

"The Museum robots are basic," he said. "Refurbished models. Antiquated, low-budget."

"Figures," I said. "And there are no Visitors!"

"The Museum's almost defunct; a forgotten trend. No longer on the tourist trail."

"Like I said, I remember almost nothing. See that—" I pointed to the fly-fishing tube. "An L.L. Bean fly-fishing rod and reel, travel size. From my supposed Worldly Possessions box. That thing, oddly, made me remember going fly-fishing. I used to like it a lot. I recall going on trips around the country, fishing for different species—trout, bass, walleye, even ocean fish."

"Do you remember your research? Or anything about a satellite station?"

"Research? Into what?" I had to laugh. "I'm pretty sure I wasn't a scientist or the scientific type. I have no memory of any satellite stations."

"Did you ever hear about a Tetra deepfake?"

"No, I don't think so..." His questions puzzled me. I was furious that the Museum wasn't telling me anything.

"So, what happens if/when I remember everything?"

"I don't know," he said.

"Where am I? Where is this Museum located?" I glared at him.

After a pause, he said, "I'm sorry. I can't tell you that."

I kept glaring. "Are we on Earth?"

He hesitated.

"I think you should go now," I said. "This interview is useless. If the Museum wants to help me, they can start by telling me what's going on and what they know. Otherwise, I have nothing for you or them! So, get lost!"

"Okay," he stood up. "They can hear you, you know—all interviews are monitored—or maybe you already figured out that you're under 24/7 surveillance."

"So much for journalistic confidentiality!"

He went to the door. A Gort was waiting for him when it opened. "They might send me back for a follow-up," he said, "but don't count on it." He went out.

"You remind me of—" I called after him, "—a cartoon character named Jiminy Cricket!"

Almost immediately, I regretted my actions. Alienating 'Jiminy.' He was my only chance for information, face-to-face human contact, my only lifeline. I didn't even get his name. I was desperate, too desperate.

I filled out a Request for another meeting, apologized for being rude; a plea for another chance.

I fantasized about going outside or even inside, just someplace big and open—even the Grand Hall. I scribbled another desperate Request.

In the meantime, I decided to check out the fly-fishing rod and reel. I took the pieces out of the case and laid them out. Then, without thinking, I assembled the rod and reel, threaded the line, and attached a fly. I did this automatically, easily. I moved some furniture out of the way, pretending I was at a small stream, a trout hole. I was in the middle of casting when I spotted Guy, across the hall, standing at his window, watching, drinking coffee. He raised his cup to me. He was back! I waved and continued my imaginary fishing. I acted out catching a fish, reeling it in. Then I cast again, reeling in slowly, slowly, and pretended to find my hook empty, as if the fish got away. It was a silent movie.

Suddenly, in the middle of back-casting, my door flew open, the lights shut down, and a loud buzzing started. I froze. I must have set something off. I saw Guy start laughing. I raised the rod and the sound intensified—buzzing louder, higher-pitched. I dropped the rod to cover my ears. A rush of Gorts swarmed in, circled the door, making mechanical chatter. They worked to close the door, oblivious to the sound, as I stood dumbfounded, staring at the fishing rod, wondering what I'd done.

A Gort came over.

"STACKS," a voice said. So. There *was* a Gort who could talk.

I walked out with the fishing rod; the Gort didn't notice. Behind us, the alarm abruptly ceased, the door shut, and the other Gorts disbanded.

When we got to the Stacks, I went down an aisle, stashed the fly rod in a corner, and began browsing for fly-fishing books. I found worn-out Orvis and L.L. Bean manuals. A sudden memory came to me, like a home movie: I was in a casting competition at the L.L. Bean fishing school in Maine. I grabbed the manuals and hurried back to my room. Then it dawned on me—I'd forgotten the rod and reel.

I woke from a nap and was startled. Guy and three Gorts were scuffling, making a big commotion across the Hall. It was strange to see, so silent, soundproofed. I stood at my window, watching in disbelief. His easy chair toppled over and a curtain was torn down as the Gorts tried to restrain him. He was shouting, waving a broom. Then suddenly, he ran out of the room, the Gorts after him. He came around the corner of the Hall and straight to my window. He pressed his hands on the glass. The Gorts grabbed him. One came up from behind and jabbed him with a needle. His body went slack and he slumped to the floor. They hauled him away. Minutes later, the lights in his room shut off, the window darkened to Night Mode and the curtains closed. I lay in the dark, eyes wide open. There had to be a way out of this nightmare, for Guy too. We had to escape, together. I didn't even know him, but I couldn't imagine him disappearing.

The next Day Mode I wondered about what I'd seen. Did it really happen or was it a dream? I peered across at his diorama, the curtains were open, his room set to Day Mode. No sign of a struggle, everything intact, but empty. Guy wasn't there. If they'd replaced a torn curtain, they'd done it fast.

Another X passed. No change in Guy's empty room. I was reading the Chandler book when I glanced up at the AI kitchen window. And then it dawned on me: Marlowe lived in LA. That gave me an idea. I went to look at the window. Sky, tree, ground. The tree. It wasn't deciduous. More like a eucalyptus tree, like ones I'd seen in California, and the landscape on the way to the Museum. Maybe

I was in or near LA... I could ask the journalist, ask in a way that would tell me—if he came back.

A Memo arrived. *Re: Fly-fishing Request: N/A.* I was fed-up with N/As! I started to tear the memo to shreds when I saw a postscript: The journalist would return for a follow-up interview. Whoop-de-doo. I had doubts that another meeting with Jiminy was worth it. I was more concerned about Guy.

An X later, a Gort escorted me to the Stacks. There was a cart with a small pile of books in an aisle. The top book was *Trout Fishing in America* by Richard Brautigan. I remembered—this was one of my favorite books! A bookmark stuck out the top, so I opened to the page. Something barely visible was scribbled on the bookmark: *invisible ink.* Puzzling ... I hadn't seen the book or cart there before. I was sure I would have seen it.

Then I remembered the fishing rod and rushed over to where I'd left it. It was gone.

Maybe the book had been left for me. By a Gort? But why take my fishing gear? I stuck the bookmark back in the book and took it. Then I went to Mystery and grabbed the only other Chandler, *The Long Good-bye.* On the way back I thought about it: *invisible ink* ... A kid's game. Writing secret messages in invisible ink. How to read it, make it visible?

I paced around my room, wracking my brains. Then, I thought: Heat. Mr. Coffee. I filled the pot with water, put it on the machine on the table. I set it to brew. While waiting for the coffee to heat up, I picked up the book, took the bookmark out, and set it on the table. I pretended to read. When the Ready light went on, I set the book down, poured a cup, and put the cup on the bookmark. I waited a couple of moments. Then I lifted the cup. The words were visible:

Monopoly doesn't know who you are. Who are you?
Did you ever hear about a Tetra?
101 Crustaceans?
Possum

I read it a couple times, memorized it and dropped it on the burner. It turned to ash.

Who was Possum—one of the Gorts? Or my neighbor, Guy? Did they program some Gorts to protect me? Doubtful. Or trick me? Nothing made sense. And the missing fishing rod irked me. I was tired—of everything! I just wanted to close my eyes. I plopped down on my bed.

INTERVIEW 2

The journalist returned the next day. I apologized for my rudeness.

"No problem. All this is new to you." He added, "Monopoly won't give me news of your future."

"Monopoly?"

"It used to be the government. No one really knows who's in power now—except those in power *now*. There's a lot of turnover. But this Museum is closing for good. They're going to tear it down. It's a copy of the long-gone New York City Main Library. Very few people read anymore."

I sat at the table, Jiminy took the easy chair again. So, Monopoly was my captor. Why? The message ... might make sense.

"They don't know much about you," he said. "They think you might be faking amnesia."

"What?" I was astounded. "Great. Something's wrong with the Monopoly's memory too? Nobody remembers anything."

"Probably one reason I'm here. To jog your memory, elicit information. Interest in Returned people has diminished over the years. Current sapiens don't really care about historical humans. You're probably an 'authentic' human—biological. Maybe even born from human parents."

"So, what's going to happen to me?" I said. "I don't want to stay here!"

"I don't know, journalists don't get much to go on. Especially if it's classified. In the past, Returned species could move on—transfer to another planet or satellite station—where most living things are, since the planetary migrations."

"Planetary migrations?"

"After your time, Earth became uninhabitable unless you lived in a bunker. Only wealthy citizens could afford it. But they left too; lack of entertainment mostly. Some travel back for exclusive parties, vacations, private hunting trips for the handful of species not already extinct. There are planet colonies for the mega-wealthy elite. The Moon is already over-populated. The *Times* office is there." He paused, thinking, and then said, "Earth is a dead planet in so many ways, a lost cause for a long time. Used mostly for Farm Labs, genetically produced food, run by robots, worked by refugees. Tragic, since it used to be home to so many ... You'll probably get transferred."

"Where?" I said. So I was on Earth.

"I don't know. Classified. A lot of regular citizens live in satellite housing, space stations, constructed moons. There's constant exploration to look for new habitats. They sign up convicts and refugees, in case the expedition fails. Almost everyone left Earth, even the ones living in bunkers."

I offered him a coffee.

"No thanks," he said. "So do you have any more questions for me?"

"I want to get out of here. Can you help me?"

"I'm sorry but I don't make Monopoly decisions. Far from it. Returnees have escaped from here, so security is vigilant now."

"Are there any humans working here? Or just robots?"

"Robots. There might be one hybrid, a humanoid or part human here to oversee. I don't know. All of my Museum contact has been through robots or cyber transmissions."

"So," I hesitated to ask, not sure I wanted to know, "are there any real humans left?"

"The majority are hybrids now: clone/AI/manufac-tured/mutated/enhanced—" He laughed again. "I used to call my mom 'The Womb' as a joke. Now that's how they refer to all birth sources."

"The fly-fishing," I said. "I have vague memories of doing demos. Maybe I was an instructor. Not a scientist. It's odd. They gave me the wrong Time Capsule."

"I doubt it," he said. "Identification is verified by DNA."

I got my writing and handed it to him. "Some things I wrote on my first day here. I don't know what any of it means; a memory, a nightmare or what."

"Okay, I'll take a look," Jiminy said. "Do you still have the Time Capsule?"

"Yeah, in my Worldly Possessions box."

"Can I take a look?"

I got the box out and opened it. Jiminy took out the Etch-A-Sketch.

"It's an Old Millennium toy. Vintage," I said. "Maybe I had one as a kid but—"

Then he took out the folded hat, opened it and put it on.

I laughed. "Called an umbrella hat, for shade. This one's an odd color—hey, it matches your coat."

He picked up the Etch-A-Sketch, fiddled with the knobs and turned it to me. **IBEX?**

Oddly, I recognized the word.

He shook it and the word dissolved.

Jiminy knows something, I thought, more than he's saying. But I decided to play dumb. "I don't know."

Jiminy paused, touched his ear. "An incoming message." He listened and turned back to me. "I'm not supposed to waste time on general history. My assignment is *your* previous life and memories."

"There's a pair of glasses too." I reached for the case with the lettering and silhouette. I read: "X-ray glasses, See through anything!" I put them on. "Another toy. They're opaque, though, too dark to see anything."

"Let me see," he said. "Let's trade."

He stood up and put the glasses on, still wearing the hat. I put on his spectacles. We laughed.

"Jiminy Cricket," I said, "A classic cartoon character, a talking cricket. He sang songs too. Big eyes and spectacles. And a top hat. He was supposed to teach this puppet kid Pinocchio to have a conscience, to distinguish between good and evil so that he would become a real human."

He laughed, "Funny name."

"What's your real name?"

"... Just call me Jiminy," he said. "So did the puppet kid become human?"

"In some endings. In other versions, Pinocchio blew it."

"You're sure you don't remember a Tetra?"

"No." Now I was really puzzled, baffled, and still suspicious. He'd asked about a Tetra before. The note from Possum asked the same question.

"There's a guy in a room across the hall," I said. "I saw him once. Do you know who he is?"

He took off the glasses and went to the window. I followed and pointed to Guy's closed curtain.

"No idea. Monopoly didn't mention him."

"I've had zero contact with him. He went crazy the other day and it took four Gorts, I mean, guards, to restrain him. They took him out of the room. His room's been vacant since." I went on, "We waved at each other when he first got here. I want to meet him but I doubt they'll let us. I'm worried what will happen to him."

He frowned. "They'll terminate him if he's an AI robot, some kind of clone hybrid, or a privately manufactured alien. They have no use for those. They'll only transfer him if he's a Returnee."

"But—I think he's human," I said, alarmed. "He looks human. Can they really just kill off someone like that—human or hybrid—?"

"Chances are he'll try to escape," Jiminy said. "Terminal ones usually make a run for it."

"I wish I'd never won the Lotto. The future ..." I shook my head.

"There's rumors that some escapees were never found. Unverified." Jiminy paused, touched his ear again, "Another message." He listened, then stood up. He took off the umbrella hat and put it in his pocket. "I have to leave now ... Can I borrow your box? I can use it for the article. Museum staff will okay it."

"Why write an article about me?" I said quickly. I didn't want him to leave.

"The Lost Returnee, that's the topic. Not much interest, but Monopoly hired me. You're the last of the original Lottery winners. There were less than a hundred. All biological humans. But there's no trace of any of them now—except you. Maybe they only Returned once. Anyway, trends last about an hour. Citizens return all the time now, mainly ones with deep pockets, coming back over and over. They want to live forever. Everlasting Life travelers, Revival tourists."

"I don't think I want to come back again," I said. "Here's your glasses." I held them out to him. He swapped glasses, set the X-ray ones in the box. Then he picked up the fishing tube and glanced inside.

"It's empty," I said. He dropped it in the box and started toward the door.

"Why don't you take off your coat—stay a minute—?" I said, desperate for him to stay.

He stopped and turned, hesitated. Then he set the box on the floor, took off his coat and hung it on a hook by the door. He reached into the box and held up the X-ray glasses. "Might come in handy," and tucked them in his coat pocket. "I'll return your box next time. They authorized three visits for the interview."

"You're the first person I've talked to since I got here."

"I know." He looked at me sadly. "Think of more questions if you want." He picked up the box and walked out the door.

I wanted to warn Guy or Possum, whatever his name was. But how? I filled out a Request to meet him. I doubted it would work. I had to come up with something. I could still see his handprints on my window.

Then, surprise—the next X, Guy was back in his room, making coffee. I hurried to my front window. He turned, I waved at him. He started toward the window but his door opened suddenly. A Gort. Guy turned and the Gort escorted him out. The door shut.

If what Jiminy said was true, there wasn't much time. I decided to scour the Stacks for info on Monopoly. Not much to choose from but maybe I'd find something. Jiminy didn't return. Xs went by. He'd forgotten his coat.

TIME CAPSULE

After the interview, Jiminy returned to his trailer, parked behind the Museum. He set Lotto's possessions box down and put aside the page with her writing. He took out the Time Capsule. If he was going to open it, the time had come to activate the trailer's surveillance buffer. A risky decision. He'd installed it incognito over the course of a year and activated it only once, as a test. The test worked but time was short—Monopoly surveillance would notice a gap in the digital terrain in an hour, if not sooner. Buffers were illegal, of course: "Illegal to evade or deflect Monopoly surveillance; a criminal security breach." So far, he'd written very little. A page lay on the table:

The Lost Returnee

States stretch across the globe. All art is illegal, banned by Monopoly, the anonymous conglomerate running the world. Bootleg art exists; suspects thrown in jail. Paintings, bassoons, tutus compressed into landfill. Live music, a crime.

Artists started banding together haphazardly, forming a union—The Illini Union—and went on a global strike. An underground subculture sprang up. Monopoly-controlled media dubbed it an 'Art Ghetto.' Then Monopoly evicted the Art Ghetto. Off-limits. And replaced it with a Monopoly Virtuosity Art Theme Park V™ a mall, a wall-to-wall tourist trap. Art clones of the dead masters. Virtual Rembrandt holding court in a café, initialing three or four masterpieces a day. "Or join (AI) Baudelaire as he pens famous passages of **Les Fleurs du Mal** in a rustic wine bar..." as advertised in the brochures.

V™ Virtual music was created as an exception to the ban, designed to slip through legal loopholes since it only exists when the listener listens. Sound bytes produced exclusively on the Virtuosity™ platform, sold to listeners and concert audiences in V™ listening canteens and megaplex screens. One byte, one play. When a byte ends you turn in your headgear or... pay to hear it just one more time! Each time you play, you pay.

Monopoly encompasses a landscape of dissolving boundaries, coups, civil wars, insurrections, insurgencies, mutinies, uprisings—a network of militias, cartels, false prophets, secret societies, corporate-government syndicates. Fallout from disasters, i.e., famine, extreme tornados, floods, temperatures, boiling oceans, disappearing geography, species extinction—added to the alphabet soup. Monopoly, the global powerhouse. Monopoly rules the world.

Jiminy picked up the Time Capsule and turned it to the lock code input. He really hoped his code worked; he'd spent so much time calculating, trying to figure it out—and he didn't know how many wrong tries he would get. If he could get it open, the Capsule would give him the story. He took a breath and input a sequence. A tiny pause, then a click. He let out a laugh. The canister was open! He removed the cap, peered in, and pulled out a rolled-up file, labeled *Monopoly – Classified: The Illini Union*.

The file pages seemed random. He set his timer for twenty-five minutes. If he ran out of time, he'd finish later. He started reading.

UNKNOWN SOURCE

I hadn't been to NYC in years, renamed New New York. Uh-huh. The first place to check was the garage, Edit's old studio. I hopped on the Hamster (aka the Transit Runner). After a couple stops, I was approached by a Stop Salesman—I think. I'd never actually encountered one before, but something was off about the jolly stranger who sidled up to me to chat. Ingratiatingly syrupy.

The purpose of a Stop Salesman is to sell you on the idea of getting off at the next stop. Say you're headed to the airport, going to Rio de Janeiro. It's their job to convince you to get off at 53rd and 9th Ave. Or you're on your way to Lex and 23rd. They convince you to get off and shop. The Stoppers are humans or clones with an Influencer Enhancement, trained by Monopoly to use incentives, by questioning self-worth, installing doubt—by creating a hole that needs filling. Rumors spread that they used hypnosis too. So I avoided eye contact, and at the next stop, I hesitated, and made a sudden dash for the exit. I didn't think he'd follow me, but I took a circuitous route anyway and stopped at a Listening Kiosk. I asked for five minutes, gear and a chart. A blank-faced clerk passed me the goods.

"Start a tab, I'll pay by thumbprint," I lied. "Expense account."

Another clerk sidled up. A girl with a black wig, a big head and even bigger smile. "Hi, what do you think of Number 10?"

I tried to step away. She blocked me.

"Ten is rising fast," she said. "It's got a lyric quality with a *super* mix of R & B, cyber rap and Adult Listening. Personally, I think the rating's *high*—it's not all *that* dangerous—but it does have a *killer* cringe factor. It's climbing fast ..."

Another Stop Sales persona or wannabe, probably on an AI feed. I snatched the chart from her hand, headed to a bubble chair, and plopped down. I put on the gear, goggles, and scanned the chart. *Not* Number Ten. I picked one called *Jungle Book,* a supposed bootleg, and keyed in.

Now I'm walking through a summer landscape, the dog days of an Indian summer in Central Park. Leaves swirl in circles in the thick heat, swishing as I walk through them. I pick one up. Geez, this is low budget. The leaf has no veins, no color gradations. I let it drop. Swishing leaves again, a sampled loop that reminds me of a washing machine. Then a sudden orchestral swell, a dramatic pause, and the band and vocals start:

> *I feel sorry*
> *for that dog*
> *he's got a drunken owner*
> *and he chews a bib for his supper*
> *and I feel sorry for that dog*
> *I feel sorry*
> *for these fish*
> *they swim between glass walls*
> *and my head is a rut*
> *and I fear it may never break apart*
> *it's a thousand degrees*
> *and there's a million dead leaves*
> *I feel sorry for that camel*

she walks the isthmus back and forth
and I fear she may never change course
and I fear we may never change course
it's a thousand degrees
and there's a million dead leaves

I stopped in my tracks; it was Edit and his band, 101 Crustaceans. But how was this possible? I checked the Top 10 list for the band name: N/A. The lyrics were his, but the voice was all wrong. An algorithm V™ impersonation or maybe they just stole it. The cheap AI landscape, the swirling leaves. I keyed out, removed the gear, and just sat there. Ludicrous. This was a whole new can of worms. Now I really wanted to find him.

I returned the gear to the counter; the clerk was cueing monitors along the wall. I looked up. Soldiers, mercenaries, a militia—no uniforms—somewhere. A captive person, blindfolded, was being forced to sit under a scraggly tree. Noise, shouting—the man turns over, his hands and feet tied. More shouting. He starts to curl up and they prop him back up against the tree, facing front. A guy enters the frame, his back to the camera, and shoots: pop pop pop. The camera zooms to a close-up of the man's imploded face—shattered teeth, his cheek a hole, his mouth as big as a dog's—panting for breath, *dying in real time?*

I was stunned. "Is this real? Live?"

"Yeah, real," the clerk said flatly.

"Yeah," the girl with the black wig, piped in. "It's one of those viral clips where a guy gets shot in the face."

The world was turning into a horror movie. I pretended to swipe my print, then made a beeline for the exit. My shadow disappeared. More weather manipulation, lighting 'adjustments,' another digital trend by some Monopoly Affiliate. Then my ears started ringing. Something was up with my Plate, interfering. Too much ambient noise in the city; I wasn't used to it.

The garage studio had to be close by. I started speed-walking the blocks, my hands over my ears. I turned onto 24th Street, the buildings familiar, covered in pigeon-shit. Pigeons had become so rampant that entire buildings got snowed under. Then people tried to simulate the effect for security reasons: nausea. Midway up the block, I saw the garage. Unmarked green double doors, upstairs windows painted black, a *For Sale* sign. This was the place. I pressed the buzzer, a circle with a half-moon. Nothing. I pressed again, waited. Still nothing. I leaned down to the mail slot, lifted the lid and yelled. No answer. The building was dead silent. I decided to check the hospital.

Jiminy had plenty of questions but he kept reading, more from the **Unknown Source.**

The Illini Union started as a joke—some pals at the University of Illinois (Champaign-Urbana Campus) came up with. Edit told a story about an elementary school teacher who had a habit of putting 'ini' at the end of words. "Do you want a snackini before your napini?" Then the Prof started calling people "Inis," and soon people were adding ini as a suffix to their names. The gag was never meant to spontaneously combust into an underground Movement or Global Artists' Strike.

Now, years later, Edit was Wanted by Monopoly V™ for supposed breach of contract, though he'd never signed one. His band, 101 Crustaceans, had been appropriated by V™. They wanted to sign him, and he'd agreed to keep them off his back, but kept putting it off. He was getting more and more annoyed by all their pestering and gimmicks: lip-syncing, vocal/instrument enhancement, cheap videos—to the point he didn't recognize his songs after being shredded by the V™ hit-maker machinery/processor. He wanted to play live.

Edit always kept a low profile. But Monopoly had gone to a lot of trouble to find him, kept trying, and just wouldn't give up. Finally, he just wanted out. He enlisted his pals in a scheme to escape, starting with Rich. They'd grown up together. "He's the guy I get all my ideas from, my best ideas," Edit said.

The **Unknown Source** ... Jiminy paused, thinking.

The next document was signed by **Rich.**

I was practicing a glide onto the Brooklyn Bridge Anchorage, after executing a parachute jump from an air taxi onto the condemned Trump Tower rooftop.

My grandma, Katie, was born in old NYC, a kooky type and theater techie. She left me a document of the Anchorage: the edifice on the East River/Brooklyn side, which holds the bridge up; a solid stone labyrinth of towering chambers. The document was a diagram of the bridge circuitry entwined with the NYC main power station. She and Stella, a lighting designer, were hired back in the day to install a lighting grid for an Anchorage Arts Festival. Nobody had a chart, since it was the first bridge built in NYC.

The core power box was in a sub-sub-basement, a mile of zigzag cutbacks below ground. Digital devices were useless. The stone edifice was just too thick. So, the women used umpire whistles and a code, an idea they got watching a Yankees doubleheader. Stella, stationed below at the core box, plugged and unplugged cables to circuits, as Katie, in the catacombs above, tooted her whistle when a bulb went on. Stella whistled back to confirm the correct circuit was marked and mapped. They worked 24/7 for a week to complete the only Brooklyn Bridge power blueprint. Knowing what it was worth, they kept it secret.

Katie gave it to me just before she died. And Monopoly wanted it.

I maintain regular jobs and deliver 'stuff'—usually illegal art, to rich people I never meet. (Sales are brokered by dealers.) I cut a deal with Monopoly and handed over the blueprint, altered of course, in exchange for a global travel pass. It's much easier to operate undetected right under Monopoly's nose, in plain sight.

The Prof used his chemistry set to make an experimental potion to counter Monopoly brain scans in case of arrest, scrambling brain matter like eggs. The upside was that this "ingestible scrambler apparatus" was only temporary, the downside: unknown side effects.

I wanted to be an explorer since I was a kid. I took up parachuting, hang-gliding, bungi jumping, cave diving, hiking, climbing—rocks, mountains, buildings—along with a secret club of like-minded fellow travelers named Possum.

Playing possum. I feel a bittersweet twinge when the now-extinct marsupial mammal comes to mind. Studying its metabolic mechanisms, I figured out how to play dead. Job reviews describe me as a nondescript unsociable dullard who sleeps on the job.

Two tasks: rigging sites for firework decoys and instigating a city-wide temporary blackout. I know the streets and alleys of NYC like the back of my hand. So, when I got a postcard from my oldest friend, Edit, I jumped at the chance

Jiminy picked up the next document in the pile, intrigued.

"What's the opposite of vital?" That's what I said to my parole officer. I got eight to fifteen in a mini-max, months not years. But the P.O. didn't know that.

"Professor of chemistry," the P.O. read. "D. J. Mendel,

a.k.a. 'The Prof' Campus pharmaceutical sales, manufacturing. Fifteen years."

"*Alleged* pharmaceutical sales. College crowd went for weed. Monopoly set me up." I tried faking the con lingo, sort of.

"Kingpin of an illegal union, it says."

"That's pure fiction. I was let out on parole with a bracelet. So," I repeat, "what's the opposite of vital?"

The P.O. looked at me. "I know it's awful out there, Darren—? but jail is no spaceship to Mars."

I pulled out a laser pen and aimed it right between his eyes. Unfortunately, the P.O. was an apocalypse survivalist. Weekends at Vegas casinos and online Sports Betting. Gambling: that was his religion, plus stockpiling bitcoin and probably WMD in his backyard. He was heavily in debt. I knew it and he knew I knew. I was saving it up for a favor he wouldn't be able to refuse.

"Go ahead, Denny. Beam me," he said. "The End is at Hand."

"Listen," I said in a fake pleading voice, "The only good thing out there is—" I waved my cigar in the air. "I'll do chemistry—and you call me whatever you want."

The P.O. blinked. "How long's it been?"

I lied. I told him two years. It was really two weeks.

A deal was cut. Officially odd jobs with my chemistry set. Unofficially, I'd finger Illini Union members. But I just made up names and identities, in exchange for re-incarceration: access to a state-of-the-art chem lab, room and board, for me and Alcatraz, my pet parrot, Cuban cigars, and art rehab: a glorious Life Drawing tutorial with live models. One model was even game to sneak messages out for me. I copied the Old Masters. Monopoly went for it: create a portal into the authentic forgeries market. "Everyone's happy." I smiled, putting on an act.

"Those were the days," I'd blabber. "None of those trendy misfits appreciate true artistry. Way back then it was a new Elizabethan Age—every day veritable masterpieces washed up on our doorsteps from foreign shores. Masterpieces washing up on our beaches, by God. What it must have felt like to be alive then!"

I admit, I laid it on pretty thick. But the job buzz wore off fast anyway, once I realized how much work they wanted out of me.

"The truth is, Al," I told my bird, "I like art."

Alcatraz peeped a couple times. I nodded, fired up a stogey, and reclined on my artist model divan. I was blowing smoke rings when the memo arrived: a ticker tape scrolling across the wall screen:

To: Professor Mendel...aka D.J. Mendel, Danny J. Re: Work Order# 13,339...I.D.
Verification: Human or humanoid
Terrorist art dealer, Strike organizer
Last known location: NNYC Mini-Max.
Authorized, Monopoly NNYC: Order to
Work: Report to Four Gated City, aka No Man's Land/Artists Ghetto, NNYC.

Description: Night crew. Fill potholes.
Patch water main on Canal Street, three blocks, east
to west. Hours: 9 p.m. to 6 a.m. only. No day hours,
by unanimous City Council decree. End date: N/A.

That's a good one/Hah! That crew had been jackhammer-
ing, slicing, digging, refilling, repaving the street for ten
years. 'Unanticipated Delays,' snafus, accidents, sewer
pipe explosions, sliced cables—threats and hostile ac-
tion from local tenants trying to sleep.

⋯ YOU WILL BE OPERATING A SHOVEL ⋯

Alcatraz started parroting the read-out: **"Operating
a shovel. A shovel. A shovel."**

I tossed the cigar and threw my arms in the air in
disgust.

⋯ REQUEST CONFIRMATION ⋯

Luckily, I'd gotten a postcard. It read: "The worms
know, yeah, the worms know best."

So far so good. I'd gotten lab access inside, set up
a network. And now I'd make the furlough work in our
favor too. I winked at Alcatraz. And I swear Alcatraz
winked at the surveillance camera.

PROF

Next, Jiminy read another page by the **Unknown Source.**

Edit worked the graveyard shift at a hospital in Jersey. His job was to deliver blood samples to the lab for testing. When asked why he volunteered for the skeleton crew, he said, "It's quiet and I can think. Nobody bothers me. The patients are all asleep or …"

He could let his mind wander as he made the rounds to the wards. He worked holidays too. The place was deserted, the pay double, and the cafeteria turkey plate wasn't bad. And there was the chapel.

They gave him a keycard to the hospital chapel. Hardly anyone ever went in there. So, the chapel became his special hide-out. There was a humongous, towering organ with an ornate, tiered keyboard. Pressing the pedals— the sound was encompassing, reverberating all around, like playing a giant's toy.

The last time I found him, he was printing song lyrics on a copier and cutting them into small squares.

"You can just keep reducing and reducing," he said. "I gave Rich one the other day and the print was so small he couldn't read it. You can keep reducing till there's nothing there. It's very tempting."

MONOPOLY AUDIO SURVEILLANCE – CLANDESTINE MEETING I

Rich: "Here's the week's headlines. (*reading*) There's been a total global power failure. Global gridlock. Possible alien sightings by Parks and Recreation, who are now conducting Operation Straw Alert and wearing undercover camouflage to blend in with the grass. Except, one source said they spotted an alien sporting stolen camouflage."

Prof: "Nothing's working, Ha. Wrenches in the works. (*chuckles*) Just hoaxes."

Rich: "Sources say the power outage is on account of a giant squid that got stuck in the water main. They're searching for it. They sent a camera down, tied to a monkey but discovered that the camera's not waterproof. And monkeys can't breathe underwater. They've got it strapped to a porpoise now."

Prof: "But Alcatraz is gone."

Dave: "That's your dead bird in the shoebox?"

Prof: "Only animals are capable of unconditional love. We're ruining the planet. I feel sorry for the animals; they had nothing to do with it."

Dave: "People always get greedy."

Rich (*reading again*): "Styrofoam bubbles and tumbleweed. Tumbleweed—its loose, all over the city—fender benders, traffic jams. It rolls sideways when nobody's looking. Kids love to chase it. They sell it secondhand in the Cloud."

Sound of someone entering.

Rich: "Hey, long time, no see."

Unknown Subject: "I got a postcard but missed the concert. Any sightings?"

Prof: "Last we heard, he went down a manhole downtown."

Rich: "Another alien sighting! (*still reading, laughs*) National Tourist Board's in a quandary over which brochures to stock. *Post* says: 'Art underground excavation site to become landfill.'"

Unknown Subject: "Hey, I found something. What's this?"

Prof: "Coat and hat set. They sell the hat in dollar stores. I concocted a special paint, mixed with a favorite Gobi species' DNA. Try them out."

Unknown Subject: (*laughter*) "Oh ... I get it now. Thanks."

Rich: "Monopoly's spreading rumors: Edit in prison, abducted ... Quote: 'Blackout caused by an underground terrorist band.' And 'Illini Union scam uncovered! Checkmate.'"

Dave: "What's Checkmate?"

Uknown Subject: "Did we meet before? You look like a Stop Salesman I saw on the Hamster."

Dave: "I doubt it ... I'd never use that cover. I joined recently."

Unknown Subject: ... "Or maybe you were at the Animatron Mall—?"

Dave: "Doubt it."

Silence.

Prof: "The worms know. Yeah, the worms know best. You know that quote, Dave?"

Silence.

Dave: "So, about Checkmate—?"

Rich: "Online company offering the perfect mate.

People describe their perfect mate in an online form and receive it via Fed Ex. Checkmate designs their significant other to their specifications, a personalized perfect fantasy. Consumers can purchase the 3-D object of desire, free shipping included. Orders flooded the site the first day and it crashed. By the time the desired orders were delivered, they'd already made a killing. The only problem was, when people opened their package, they discovered that Checkmate followed their specifications literally—to the letter. People received reclining chairs, light bulbs, artificial plants, canning jars, broken tape-recorders, even bathtubs. Some customers just got a flash drive with data, like Wordle puzzles. Very high price tag. Checkmate vanished, consumers were enraged—for getting exactly what they described—like a teapot. Major backlash. Monopoly blamed the Illini Union, issued warrants."

Prof: "Let me see that. (*paper shuffling, then reads*) Over 50 percent of the planet's original species extinct. Mutant species are able to morph and mutate like viruses. Dinosaur-size rats, mega-octopuses and jellyfish. There's a surge in life-size bugs and spiders too. And pigeons, especially in Old New New York."

Rich: "A lot of avatars too."

Dave: "Or wannabes ... Any word on 99?

Rich: "Checked himself into a hospital in Paris to see a sexy nurse."

Uknown Subject: "I'm heading out now," (laughs) "on the road to hell—"

Dave: "What road to hell?"

Prof: "Wait—something you should know. The Illini Union, the Inis were a myth—that Monopoly created. They put out rumors: Inis are born in test tubes with biological DNA or cloned. And Plates are high-end enhancements for a select few. Monopoly also issued warnings: that they'd erase or infect the Plates with toxins—to keep Inis under control or make them *think* so. Fear mongering. But so far, scientists say that if a Plate's erased, there *might* be memory loss or not. It's 50-50. We pretty much end up with that kind of choice anyway."

Dave: "Free will is a myth."

Unknown Subject: "50-50. Well, fingers crossed."

Prof: "Here's to free time on the planet, short as it is. No one controls Time."

Dave: "See you in the Future!"

Unknown Subject: "What? Nobody knows how this will end ..."

Sound of exit.

[RECORDED BY UNDERCOVER OPERATIVE. NOTE: IDENTIFY UNKNOWN SUBJECT.]

MONOPOLY AUDIO SURVEILLANCE — CLANDESTINE MEETING II

Prof: "She saw him on the Hamster as a Stop Salesman, but he denied it, lied—he's a mole—"

Sound of door opening.

Rich: "Which do you want first, the bad news or the terrible news?"

Door closes.

Dave: "What happened? What's going on?"

Rich: "Edit once said he liked the idea of people living in a cave someplace, making music he'd never hear."

Dave: "That's where we are now ... Dying in a cave."

Silence.

Prof: "... What happened to the Module, Dave? Tell us."

Dave: "What? I don't get it."

Prof: "How could you—you're a Stop Salesman. You never got a postcard."

Pause.

Dave: "I got arrested just like everybody else!"

Rich: "And let go ... Did they let you go with enhancements—?"

Dave: ... "There were *a lot* of rumors."

Rich: "Cash bounty for Edit, plus sell the Module?"

Prof: "Decoy Dave. How do you live without a self?"

Dave: "... Yeah? Okay. I cut a deal. Man, I had to sign with them. (*Silence*) My career was on the skids ... I've got a new place, a better view. Now, for once, I get to win. And feel like a million bucks!"

Rich: "Your world is not my world. You're a loser."

Dave: "Maybe in the Old Millennium, but not in the New one: *New New York* is different!"

Prof: "Without the Module, we've got nothing, zero.

They'll crash her plate. All the songs will disappear and maybe her memory. Gone."

Rich: "Yep. Everything gets *virtually* stolen by Monopoly. Erased."

Dave: "That happens to everybody."

(*Door slams, then re-opens.*)

Dave: "People. I like their mask more than what's underneath."

(*Door slams again.*)

Prof: "Dave snitched. Sold us out."

Rich: "Here's something– Edit left this– *Blue Light*. The band's last concert and the last song. When it ended, the tour vanished into thin air."

Prof: "We're on Monopoly's radar now. Time to clear out."

[ASSIGNMENT TERMINATED — MONOPOLY MOLE/ UNDERCOVER OPERATIVE COVER BLOWN.]

Blue Light

once I was in a blue light
where things strange things
stood out in relief
like a chain stuck in a road
and a snail on a fence
and I thought
what I didn't know has really hurt me
once I was in the North Woods

and I saw a blue heron
drink from a stream
and a woodchuck crossing a log bridge
in a rainstorm of doodads
and I thought
what you don't know can really hurt you
once I slipped in time
to before I was born
and I saw a man in a shop
standing at a printing press
he was pulling out blueprints
and each as it touched his hand
would turn into a lion
and some of the lions had wings
soon the whole room was full of lions
flying in circles near the ceiling
banging off the walls
'cause the room was tight
until one broke free and flew up
through the skylight and into the night
and the man looked at me and said
"that was you"
what you don't know can really hurt you
I'm a dark light in the night sky
What you don't know can really hurt you

MONOPOLY SATELLITE SURVEILLANCE

Visual of an Unknown Entity traveling south across Gobi dune-scape, in heavy sand turbulence. Unknown Entity traverses dunes, disappears, reappears. Arrives at a small shed, approximately one hour later.

A second figure, an Unidentified Human, exits the shed, wearing a dayglow green vest, face obscured by a sun hat. Freeze frame. The U-Human re-enters the shed, followed by the U-Entity. Moments later, the U-Entity exits the shed and disappears over a dune, in the direction of Ulan Bator. The U-Human exits the shed with an object (watering can) and waters a plot of stalks. UH returns the can to the shed and heads toward the Gobi Research Station on a sandboard. UH arrives at the research station, enters. Later, close to sunset, UH exits the station, stands outside. Monopoly arrest team enroute. Final destination/location of UE unknown.

[PROBABLE IDENTITIES: UNIDENTIFIED HUMAN: WHO? — UNKNOWN ENTITY: POSSIBLE GOBI IBEX OR MUTANT-ENLARGED JERBOA]

All Sewn Up

long mud crawl
earth suck scream
chain gasp breath
blasted light

need crazed howl
mouth pry clamp
thumping hump
fierce tut tut
coo grub stunt
crush routine
shame body split
soar swirl thunk
and mad rushes to embrace
the newest spike in the collar
before it could even crawl
it was
all sewn up

Jiminy was putting the tiny pieces of the lyrics together when the timer went off. Just a few pages to go; he'd have to finish later. He locked the file back in the capsule and deactivated the trailer buffer. He sat thinking, wondering about gaps in the story, about how much Monopoly knew, then and now. Most of it read like stories or a diary, and this intrigued him, but who was the storyteller and who was the listener? Some of the puzzle pieces were falling into place. He read the page Lotto had given him. And then he began writing.

FREE FALL

I wondered if Jiminy would ever return. I Xed another day on my calendar. My life as a vintage specimen. I couldn't imagine this for the rest of my life ... No. There had to be some way to break out. I considered bribing Allegra, the Gorts were too simple. But it would only work if her survival felt threatened. Early on, AI algorithms had figured out how to "survive," no matter what. That was their sole instinct. They became adept at sneaking around or subverting any code that would trigger their Off switch and end them. I'd started to try out prompts to fool the Gorts, like anti-emojis, to send them into a tailspin. But, so far, the only emoji that seemed to give them pause was one that looked like them. Anyway, it was just a theory.

The lights and windows faded to Night Mode and the curtains closed. I put on my sleepwear (one of the jumpsuits I'd cut in half), got into bed, and closed my eyes.

A strange noise woke me. I sat up and looked around in the dark. The door to my room was open. I couldn't believe it. I went to look. All of the lights were off in the Grand Hall, maybe the entire Museum was dark. I grabbed my sneakers, put them on, took Jiminy's coat from the hook next to the door, and put that on too. Then I stepped into the hall. Dead silence. I knew the way to the Stacks by heart. I'd go there, maybe find a way out. I started a slow jog, stepping as quietly as possible.

I didn't know what was happening, but I didn't want to get caught outside my room. And wearing Jiminy's coat—surveillance might think that I was him. The doors to the Stacks were open. I stopped and listened. Nothing. I started walking past the tables, checking the aisles. I froze. Something, a shape, was at one of the tables. I went up close. Guy! Guy, slumped over the top.

I touched, then squeezed his arm. Nothing. I leaned close to his ear. "Hey—" I whispered. He didn't budge. I felt his neck for a pulse. He was alive. I poked him. No response.

What was he doing here? He was holding something, a penlight. I covered it with my hand, pressed it on. There was a water bottle and an Etch-A-Sketch, with words on it:

TRAVEL + FLY ROD
CORNER L MANHOLE
GLASSES ON
CU F2

I heard a sudden noise, an alarm buzzing—and froze. I couldn't stay there. I shook the Sketch, grabbed the bottle, flicked off the pen, and made a beeline toward the back of the room. Stuffing the bottle and Sketch in my pockets, I continued past aisles and, at Travel—a shelf at the end stood askew. As I moved closer, I noticed a door behind it was wedged open—with my fishing tube?? No time to think about it. The buzzing was getting louder, I could hear Gorts, noises, a commotion moving toward the Stacks.

"Here! Wake him. Get him up!" I heard Allegra shouting orders.

Quickly, I squeezed past the shelf and out the door. I held the door and pulled the tube out, letting it close, trying not to make a sound.

The night was dark outside. I was on a small landing, a few stairs to the street. I swung the tube over my shoulder, jumped down the stairs, and headed along the side of the building. I was almost to the corner when the whole Museum lit up in a surge of power and deafening buzzing alarms. The blackout was over.

I went around the corner, searching for the manhole in the Etch-A-Sketch message. It was mid-way up the street. I ran to it and hoisted the lid; it was heavy. Then, leaning down, I pressed the penlight on. A wall ladder. I climbed down a few rungs, reached back out, and heaved the lid over me.

I scrambled down the ladder in the dark as fast as I could. No time to waste. Deep down, I hit bottom, out of breath and scared. It was pitch black. I needed to think, just for a moment. The Etch-A-Sketch had said Glasses On. I felt around inside Jiminy's coat pockets and took out the X-ray ones he'd tried on. When I put them on, I saw day glow colored tags among layers and layers of graffiti scrawled on the circular walls and ceiling, the arc of a concrete tunnel. Maybe an abandoned water main. Old-timey graffiti murals; abstract and figurative shapes, colored spirals, loops all along the sides. I jogged and speed-walked, passing the tags, which turned out to be words. Soon I realized that I was following a message inbetween tags—words written in dayglow paint. The glasses weren't X-ray vision; they were vintage Black Light—highlighting the messages.

follow tunnel end day trip

I kept going until I saw something ahead on one side: a Day-Glo circle. I slowed down to approach—a wheel—of a bicycle. A bicycle. I checked the tires. What a relief. Now I could move faster. I stood still and listened: dense silence, no noises behind me. I took off the fishing tube and coat; I couldn't ride with the coat on. A bottle fell out of the pocket. Water! I took a couple gulps. There was something else in there—the umbrella hat. I put it back, stuffed the bottle in the other pocket, and tied the coat around my waist. I swung the tube back over my shoulder and hopped on the bike. The graffitti and a front reflector kept me moving in a straight line, following slight bends in the tunnel.

hat coat east farm 2 shack CU

The words repeated as I rode.

Where was I going? Had other escapees used the tunnel, like an underground railroad. Guy—what happened to him? Was he trying to escape and help me escape too? Why? What if he got caught? What if I got caught? ... Where was I going? To a farm, a shack, and then what? I just kept pedaling, moving ahead, too afraid to stop. The biking came easy to me. Bits of memories started coming back—biking in tunnels, over canyons, along rivers, trails, roads, highways ...

And I kept thinking about Guy. If he got caught, would Monopoly send interrogators? Ship him off to some remote satellite prison? Or terminate him? Maybe they'd just close the place for good and leave him behind ... Sure.

The air in the tunnel started to feel warmer. Warm, then hot, then cold again. Maybe I was close to the end. I'd been biking a long time, hours, miles. I came around a bend and saw a small circle of light in the distance. I wanted to holler YAY Hooray—but my voice would echo. The end of the tunnel was close. I raised the glasses on top of my head and sped up. Before I reached the end, now a bright wide circle, I stopped and got off the bike. I leaned it against the wall, left the fishing tube with it, and walked to the opening.

Light and heat blasted me. I untied the coat from my waist, took the umbrella hat from the pocket and swapped it with the glasses. I put the coat and hat on. I looked out. The tunnel came out to concrete, an empty irrigation ditch, bone dry. Concrete walls angled up-wards, an overpass on one side. I scrambled up the incline ahead of me to get a look. A deserted highway stretched in both directions into the distance, like a mirage. Dust, sand, wind, microchips and the dim, polluted fog. Blasts of hot and cold wind. Behind me, the barest outline of something, maybe the place where I'd been. Maybe what used to be LA. The sun was coming up in front of me. East. Across the highway lay a sprawling valley in the weird fog. Desolate 'farmland.' No sign of life anywhere.

Squinting, I searched for a 'farm.' In a blast of hot wind, I spotted something shining, maybe a roof—in fact, several rectangular shapes. Like the warehouses I'd seen from the mansion lot. Farm labs ...? There was nothing else in sight. I had to take my chances. And I didn't want to linger on the overpass. I scrambled back down, skid-ding on the sand and concrete to the ditch. I went back to the tunnel, straight for the water bottle. I was incredibly thirsty— tempted to finish it off. But if what I'd spotted was just shadows or a mirage, I was out of luck. Guessing it was at least five miles to the farms or whatever they were. Guessing. I took off the hat and sat in the tunnel, the air felt cool in my hair. Rest for just a moment ...

I figured I should get moving, before sunrise. I had no idea what the Museum would send looking for me. I stood up, water and glasses in pockets, and swung the tube strap over my shoulder. After putting the hat back on, I crossed beneath the overpass. I climbed up on the other side of the highway and started trekking.

I don't know how much time passed, but the sky kept shifting from light to dark, as if there were clouds overhead. I couldn't tell through the foggy air, sand, and the fluctuating blasts of hot and cold wind if there were clouds. Like at the mansion lot, it felt like an ongoing eclipse of the sun. I passed more vacant foundations, decrepit swimming pools. Some were filled with plastic items, bags, toys, junk. Bright, colorful. The trash looked new—plastic—made to last forever. Several times I saw it ignite spontaneously, making small fires.

Suddenly I remembered the nightmare or memory, whatever it was, from my first night, after Restoration. I was lost, trying to get home, in some city. I didn't know where exactly. And then a childhood memory came to me, in vivid detail. Waking up at night, sitting on the stairs in the dark, thinking about death. I'd just sit there, trying to picture it: everybody gone, the cessation of being, trying to imagine Nothing.

I remembered telling a friend about it. And I got embarrassed, apologized for bringing it up.

"Oh, no problem," my friend said. "I think about death all the time. At least once a day."

And another memory popped up, of my sister. *My sister... did I have a sister?*

I remembered going to her when I was a kid, excited, telling her how I flew downstairs on my pillow in a halo of light. She looked at me and laughed. I started crying, "I did too!" and stormed off.

This led to another memory, when we were teenagers.

She said, "Remember when we were kids and you told me that you flew downstairs on your pillow—in a halo of light?"

I had to think a minute. "Oh yeah, I remember that. And you said I didn't."

"Well, I was wrong," she said. "I know you flew down there. I was just jealous. That's why I said it. I'm sorry." We both laughed.

Walking, trudging; across a flat landscape of rocks, sand, dust, and microchips—trying not to think about the distance, how far I had to go. But oddly, I felt hopeful; the 'eclipse' effect gave me cover at least. Every now and then I heard the faintest buzzing, like flies. It was the only sound, except for the wind.

Walking, walking, I started humming to myself, like I was marching to the shape in the distance. As I got closer, I could see three buildings in a row, large hangars, mega-grow houses? I stopped and just watched, to see if there was anyone, Security, around. Nobody in sight. The tunnel tags said Farm 2 shack 2; it had to be the center one. The sun was definitely coming up. I approached the building slowly and walked along one side, looking for an entrance. In back, a couple hundred yards away, an overturned rusty wind tower lay on its side, along with remnants of metal shapes stuck in the sand, and another foundation hole to one side.

I found a door in back, a sliding industrial type. I tugged and slid it open slightly. As soon as I got inside, I stopped in my tracks, completely startled. just enough to enter. Straight ahead on the far wall were piles of bodies. Piled from floor to ceiling, hundreds of them. I went closer, slowly. They didn't look human. Probably just high-end robots—various shapes, sizes, sexes, ages—with astounding detail. Out-of-commission robots. But what if there were clones or even escapee bodies in the pile? The thought made me gag. I couldn't let myself think about it. I started looking around the lab. Circuit boards, microchips, cables strewn on the floor. Metal walls, inside and out. Rows and rows of servers on one side, maybe an abandoned bitcoin mine ...? The ceiling was covered in a pattern of circuit panels and vent holes.

Shelves along the opposite wall held remnants of office/maintenance type equipment and more cyber rubble. I found some old framed photos, B/W relics of people in groups, workers, equipment, trucks. Definitely another era, very Old Millennium. One was of an ancient wooden shack. My breath caught. I stared at it. A dilapidated shack, light coming through slats in the walls. A door hung loose, an empty window frame next to it. And near the shack, a standing wind tower. This had to be the shack. I needed to go out to the tower area and look around. I headed back to the door and slid it open for a peek.

I thought I heard buzzing flies again, but didn't see any. Flies ...? Then it hit me. Drones. I scanned the sky. Something up there was heading my way. The buzzing was getting louder, so I slid the door shut, panicking. I had to hide. But where? I ran to the pile of bot bodies, searching for an opening to climb in. I yanked the hat off my head, shoved it in my pocket, and rolled one of the bodies sideways. The tube was still over my shoulder. I crawled into the pile as far as I could go and turned on my side. The drones might sense body heat, my pulse—I covered my face with a bot limb. The humming was louder now. I lay as still as possible, the bodies over me. The buzzing was coming close; the drone must have come through one of the empty vents. I breathed slowly. I sensed the drone above, circling the ceiling, then descending lower in the room, hovering over the piled bodies. Paralyzed by fear, I closed my eyes. The circling continued, the buzzing coming close, moving past, over and over.

I stayed like that for hours. Finally, the buzzing started to fade and then it was gone. I stayed still though, too afraid to move—if the drone returned...

Eventually I sensed the light changing, in between the bodies, inside the lab. I was afraid to move out of the pile, but I couldn't stay there forever. I had to come out. I'd found F2 but I had to get to the shack. At least I had a place to hide. I shimmied backwards from the pile, out of my hole, scared stiff, holding onto the fishing tube. I walked carefully along the wall of the lab to the shelf with the photo and looked at it again. Then I went to the door and listened. No buzzing flies, no sound at all. I slid the door open enough to get out and made a beeline to the tower. What was in the other buildings? Maybe I could check later.

Beyond the tower, in the distance I saw more of the same buildings. I went past another empty foundation hole. The tower lay on its side—sand and rubble, servers, circuitry scraps, microchips, a cyber trash heap. I searched around the tower and saw a busted server, a metal plate lying at an odd angle under it. I went over and pushed the server as best I could, to the side, lifting the heavy plate slightly. I kept tugging at it and saw a hole. I managed to swivel the plate sideways and knelt down to look inside. Maybe an old well. There was something dark, four or five feet down. I had to check it out. I really hoped I could get back out. I sat down and slid into the hole feet first.

The object was a rucksack.

I looked up and the plate opening I'd come through wasn't too large. I turned on my penlight, set it down, then reached up with the tube and pushed the metal plate, inching it over the hole. I set the tube down and took off my hat and coat. I was covered in sweat. Inside the rucksack was a full water canister, a small flashlight (that worked), a pocketknife, compass, three wrapped sandwiches, apples, and snack bags. And, at the bottom, an old phone message machine—totally outmoded, even in my time. Record/Playback on analog mini-reel tapes. No tape inside but the batteries worked. Go figure. I spread the coat on the floor for a picnic, gobbled down a sandwich, and guzzled some water, saving the rest for when Guy or 'CU' showed up. I leaned on the wall of the hole and stretched out my legs. Aching and exhausted, I could barely keep my eyes open. Then I started worrying.

Guy. What if he didn't make it? Global surveillance

was institutionalized even before my time, I couldn't imagine what it had become. The Old Millennium, the New Millennium, the Lost Millennium, and now—what would it be called—the Last Millennium? Whatever millennium, this would be my last. One life was enough. A wrecked desolate planet ... some legacy! And where did I think I was going? My only hope was to find some escaped Returnees ... On the other hand, one thing was for sure: I wasn't going back. Not without a fight. I closed my eyes to take a cat nap.

I don't know how long it lasted. When I woke, I could see light along the edges of the metal plate. All I could do was wait. I decided to look at the fishing rod. I removed the tube cap. But there was no fishing rod, the Time Capsule was inside. Nothing made any sense. Jiminy had taken my Worldly Possessions box and the Time Capsule ... But I was still curious about it. I turned the tube upside down and let the Capsule slide out. I looked at the code slot, stared at the numbers. I'd never figure it out. I twisted the cap anyway—and it came off. It opened! Then I saw digits on the inside of the fishing cap. They matched the code slot on the capsule. So, Jiminy or Guy or a Gort or someone had cracked the code.

Inside the capsule was a thin scroll of papers. I pulled it out, flattened the pages, and started reading by penlight. I read and it made my head spin, but I kept reading.

The Lost Returnee

It starts out. Out in the boondocks, outside Ulan Bator. Tetra Z-ini was at her Gobi Desert habitat, a satellite station for wave/vibration measurements. She was a Level One Researcher/ Enhanced (with a Plate in her head). Plates were bio-engineered, not fabricated gizmos, Receiver/Transmitters. Tetra's job was to monitor outer space—galactic matter, planetary events, star births/deaths, extraterrestrial messages. A lot of it was noise. And a lot of messages were from Earth, people pretending to be aliens or from Lonely Hearts Clubs.

Tetra had a secret garden too, hidden far out in the dunes, where she grew moonflowers. And worms. She had a small worm farm.

In addition to her Plate, Tetra had a Module, a device for surveillance/reconnaissance conducted by the host, Monopoly, to assess competitive infiltration, advantage, and maintain control. In other words, Monopoly monitored the monitor. Should either be compromised or hacked, Monopoly would crash the Module by remote, which would, in turn, erase Tetra's Plate, all data and all memory terminated and rendered useless, like a broken dish.

Edit always kept his coat on when he came over.

Finally, I asked, "Do you want to take off your coat?"

"I don't feel as though I have a right to take off my coat in somebody else's house or home!"

I remember one time, we were walking down 23rd Street and passed a Wellmart Outlet, brainchild of Monopoly pharma. Designer injestibles and injectables: micro-experiences to overcome feelings of defeat, mostly loneliness. AI devices too. I pointed to something that looked like AI-generated angel wings.

"Wings? To fly—or what?" I said.

"Sure," he said, "I'm still waiting for humans to develop a conscience."

I'd seen a Siberian Tiger at the zoo recently. I told him about it.

"There were two," I said, "but it was autumn and colder, so only one was out of the cave. The pen was a rectangle with tiers and a small pool. The tiger walked the perimeter then leaped up the tiers to a fence in back where people watched from outside. He gave a roar, pacing back and forth past them. Then he sprang down the tiers, past the pool, to the front fence. He came near, circled, and stopped, looking straight at us, holding our gaze. I wondered what he saw." Edit nodded and I continued. "On the way out, I passed an info board: only four hundred tigers left in the world! I was dumbfounded, sickened. I couldn't shake it. I couldn't stop thinking about the tigers. For the next two weeks I just walked around hating people."

"Humans," Edit said. "Not my favorite species."
The page was signed **Unknown Source.**

The Lost Returnee continued:

The escape plan was a series of decoy concerts in cities around the globe, all AI variations of the one, live, real-time Crustaceans concert in New NYC. As soon as Monopoly goon squads arrived to bust up one concert, another popped up, which kept them running behind.

Simultaneously, fireworks went off at landmarks like the Brooklyn Bridge, Eiffel Tower, Leaning Tower of Pisa, St. Louis Arch and more. At the end of the concert, Possum set off a 30-minute NYC blackout, for cover.

The Prof released hoaxes to Monopoly news media and fringe doomsayers to muddy the waters, while Monopoly claimed that the concert was a "terrorist attack by Illegals." Later on, a source leaked that the Prof was returned to prison but got released by his P.O. 'by mistake.' A Monopoly investigation revealed the Prof's entire incarceration was a con: for lab access and use of city underground tunnels while on work furlough. The P.O. denied taking a bribe but was fired anyway.

A slew of postcards was found during a search of the hospital chapel, with handwritten quotes. Edit had sent them to his pals. Monopoly was unable to decode them (probably because there was nothing to decode). The cards had a fake postmark, the date of the last concert.

1. The road to hell is paved with good intentions.
2. Life consists of being born, crawling through open country under heavy fire, and dropping into your grave.
3. The leaves are getting faker every day.
4. The worms know, yeah, the worms know best.

The Illini Cyber Crew (99, gamers & hackers) hijacked (and recycled) an antiquated clone network for the AI concerts, by temporarily hacking the Monopoly V™ concert network. Monopoly's scheduled concerts were canceled and replaced by clones of 101 Crustaceans (Edit's band). Marketing and ticket sales were initiated by hacking Influencers, who could report being hacked, or make money off it. None reported it.

The clone concerts were routed through a global Darknet, a labyrinth of DOGE scams, vigilante groups, J6 militias, cartels & dummy'legit' corporations, offshore accounts, Bitcoin chains—the best and brightest of corruption—finally passing through the cemetery gravesite of the desecrated tomb of a dictator named Putin (long dead, though he tried several times, but failed to Return). The tomb was the cyber-attack source too, an untraceable mega-loop, codenamed MAGA, a joke on ultimate hubris.

The NYC concert started in real time, cueing the server to initiate the clone concert sequence.

Tetra uploaded the songs on the playlist to random satellites long before the night of the concert, using her Plate, and signing her nickname: Tetra Z-ini. The songs were set to play on different dates and times over the next year. As soon as a song was broadcast, Monopoly scurried to shut it down—but it took real time to trace it from satellite to satellite, through a web of encryption layers. Plenty of time for listeners on Earth to make bootleg copies. The only fast way to delete the playlist was to blow up the satellites. But none of the private owners would go for that.

Monopoly media churned out conflicting reports, sightings, and tips: something went wrong, a failed escape attempt—Edit was sold out by his friends, on Death Row, or hiding out, was abducted, had cloned himself, faked his death ... was in prison, dead, or in orbit ... it was an endless rumor mill.

"He was in way over his head," Monopoly declared. But Monopoly had no idea what happened, where he'd gone. Nobody did. Nobody knew for sure, except Tetra.

The next page was an old blurry digital news clip of some guys, torn along the top, maybe the bottom half of something. Who were they? Edit and his band? I didn't recognize any of them. Maybe ... Possum? Rich = Possum. But did Guy = Rich? And Tetra ...

I kept reading.

Edit showed up at my moonflower plot in the Gobi, out of the blue. He had a back-up playlist, not knowing I didn't need it. He was leaving for good.

"You were in a dream I had," I said. "I woke up laughing."

"A dream you woke up laughing from, that's pretty good."

We swapped clothes in the shed. His bright green vest for my Ibex coat. I waited inside, for him to disappear. Then I watered the moonflowers and headed back to the station. I figured Monopoly would show up soon enough, a team would descend on the satellite station to arrest Edit—and find me. They'd probably crash the Module, erase my Plate ... But before they did, maybe I'd get a chance to watch the moonflowers bloom one last time. Maybe I'd get away too. I listened to one of his songs via satellite while I waited for Monopoly.

Free

If you don't want to be free
then just do what you always do
If you don't want to be happy

just do what you always do
If you don't want to be free
of this iron maw
then stay where you are
stay where you are
If you don't want to be happy
then do
what you always do

Tetra

FLATLINE

I stood up and pushed the metal plate covering the hole sideways. It was dark out now. I looked up at a wonder of stars, myriad stars, everywhere. It astonished me. The polluted fog was gone. I saw something—a tiny flash of light in the west. I decided to crawl back out and head back to F2, wait for Guy or—? After putting everything back in the Time Capsule and rucksack to leave there, I put on the coat and hat, and stuck the water bottle in my pocket.

Climbing out proved difficult. I started to panic again. But I had to get out. After several tries, gripping the edges of the plate and the hole, I managed to pull myself up, pushing my feet against the wall. I was scraped and dirty all over.

The sky was a starry dome. The wind was gone, replaced by a blanket of silence and random creaking noises. More flashes of light to the west in the distant sky like

... fireworks? The explosions came in random bursts and directions. A Possum decoy—? Maybe the story was repeating itself. I went slowly and checked the other buildings. One was sealed shut, the other was filled with bodies and junk like F2. Best to return to F2 and wait there. Once inside, I drank the rest of the water and stuck the bottle in between the door and the wall. If anyone opened it, the bottle would drop. I went back to my opening in the pile, rearranged a few bodies, just slightly. If the drone returned, I didn't want it to see changes. I set it up so I could lean my shoulders and head against a body and see the door, keeping another body close, for cover. I climbed into my hidey-hole to wait.

When I woke, it was light. I'd fallen asleep. Not good. I kept still and listened. Nothing. I waited a little longer, then shimmied out and stood up. Now what? Where was Guy? I tried not to panic. If only I hadn't fallen asleep! I put on the hat and went to check the door. The bottle was on the floor; someone had opened the door. Whoever it was, I'd missed them. So ... I was on my own. I'd have to keep going east. There was no turning back, unless Guy or whoever was in the well. Either way, I needed to go back, get the Time Capsule and tube. Eat something, refill my water.

I tugged the metal plate aside. No Guy. Nobody. If he'd been at F2, I'd missed him. It was time to get moving. I dropped back into the well and then I saw the Etch-A-Sketch on top of the rucksack next to the wall. The screen read:

Tunnel (an arrow going down) **Take Sack Glasses. Tags CU**

I shook it, the message dissolved. Underneath the sketch was an old B/W photo and a mini-cassette. I picked up the photo, stood up, and held it in the light. *It was me!* This made no sense. I turned it over.

Tetra

I looked at the photo again. I didn't recognize the background. I stared at it. Tetra from the scroll story ... Monopoly thought I was Tetra because the DNA matched. Tetra was me or ... a clone, cloned from me ...? Or was I the clone?

Who took the photo? ... I pulled the pages from the Time Capsule, looking for the digital clip. I stared at it. Edit. He had to be one of the people in the photo ... And then I had an intuition. What if—Edit ... *Returned and disguised? Jiminy. The journalist* ... He'd come to interview me to see if I was Tetra. Tetra, who had disappeared ... Or was my escape a Monopoly set-up? Possibilities. But now I wanted to *know*. Now I was determined to find out who I was, and if I was Tetra or who Tetra was and if I had a sister ...

I moved the rucksack aside and started digging in the sand. Maybe ten inches down, I felt something, and dug the sand away. A trapdoor. I lifted it—ladder rungs going down. I started to repack the rucksack, wondered about taking the message machine. And then I remembered the mini-cassette. I searched around for it and found it near

the Sketch. I inserted the cassette and pressed Play. I'd
read Edit's lyrics, now I heard his voice.

Flatline

the light gleams
like acetylene
on this house
in the outland
the bed clay
is a cracked hand
where all the water
disappears
and all the atmosphere
is barely breathing
and dust is sweeping
to and fro
the flies are thick as soup
and wounds are weeping
we'll not be coming here again
'cause there's a flat line
creeping through the sun
it's got a choke-hold
on everyone
guess this dustbowl lease
is already run
'cause there's a flat line
creeping through the sun

and it's so hot
in the new world order
there's no one here today
even the ghosts are gone
the barn door's banging
in the wind
the flies are glowing green
and wounds are weeping
we'll not be coming
here again
and the ants dream of the new world order

K.M. Williams writes fiction & non-fiction and creates visual art. Born and raised in the Midwest, Williams studied visual art at the Kansas City Art Institute and creative writing at Brooklyn College and She was founder, writer, and director of Kindness, Inc., a NYC experimental theater company producing over 30 plays, presented in NYC, around the US, and in Indonesia. She now lives in Kansas City, Missouri.